Duck, Duck, Porcupine!

Salina Yoon

BLOOMSBURY
NEW YORK   LONDON   OXFORD   NEW DELHI   SYDNEY

For Lily and Tansy, with love!

First published in the United States of America in May 2016
by Bloomsbury Children's Books
www.bloomsbury.com

Bloomsbury is a registered trademark of Bloomsbury Publishing Plc

For information about permission to reproduce selections from this book, write to
Permissions, Bloomsbury Children's Books, 1385 Broadway, New York, New York 10018
Bloomsbury books may be purchased for business or promotional use. For information on
bulk purchases please contact Macmillan Corporate and Premium Sales Department at
specialmarkets@macmillan.com

Library of Congress Cataloging-in-Publication Data
Names: Yoon, Salina, author.
Title: Duck, Duck, Porcupine! / Salina Yoon.
Description: New York : Bloomsbury Children's Books, 2016.
Summary: Big Duck likes to boss around her younger brother, Little Duck, and she fancies herself the leader of
their trio when joined by their gentle friend Porcupine. Little Duck does not speak yet, but through his expressions
and his actions, he shows that he has a better grasp on any situation than his older sister.
Identifiers: LCCN 2015022813
ISBN 978-1-61963-723-8 (hardcover) • ISBN 978-1-61963-812-9 (e-book) • ISBN 978-1-61963-869-3 (e-PDF)
Subjects: | CYAC: Ducks—Fiction. | Brothers and sisters—Fiction. | Porcupines—Fiction. | BISAC: JUVENILE FICTION/
Animals/Ducks, Geese, etc. | JUVENILE FICTION/Social Issues/Friendship. | JUVENILE FICTION/Family/Siblings.
Classification: LCC PZ7.Y817 Du 2016 | DDC [E]—dc23
LC record available at http://lccn.loc.gov/2015022813

Art created digitally using Adobe Photoshop
Typeset in Cronos Pro
Book design by Salina Yoon and Colleen Andrews
Printed in China by Leo Paper Products, Heshan, Guangdong
1 3 5 7 9 10 8 6 4 2

Three Short Stories

One
A Perfect Day for a Picnic

Two
I Think I Forgot Something!

Three
The Campout

One

A Perfect Day
for a Picnic

Yes it is, Big Duck!

I will get the picnic blanket.

Two

I Think I Forgot Something!

Three

The Campout

26. fishing pole
27. pots
28. pans
29. sate

59. lamp
60. root beer
61. toaster
62. cha